SOCRATES IS EVERYTHING

By Kathleen Leatherbarrow

Table of Contents

CHAPTER 1: OLYMPIC DREAMER 5

CHAPTER 2: MYSTERY GIRL 13

CHAPTER 3: A CATERPILLAR STUCK IN HER COCOON 21

CHAPTER 4: TIME FOR A CHANGE 28

CHAPTER 5: RISE OF THE PANTHERS..31

CHAPTER 6: A CHECKERED PAST...37

CHAPTER 7: AND WHAT A CHANGE! 41

CHAPTER 8: REJECTION IS UGLY 47

CHAPTER 9: PLAYING BY MYSELF 50

CHAPTER 10: NOT A GIRL!...54

CHAPTER 11: FINALLY! 61

CHAPTER 12: HEADERS MADE HAPPY 63

CHAPTER 13: THE CHALLENGE 70

CHAPTER 14: THE BIG EFFORT 72

CHAPTER 15: THE SHOE CHALLENGE 75

CHAPTER 16: A BAD DECISION 80

CHAPTER 17: CAPTURE! 87

CHAPTER 18: I LOVE SOCCER!...90

CHAPTER 19: THE AVOCADO PLAN..94

CHAPTER 20: EYE ON THE GOAL 97

CHAPTER 21: THE BIG AVOCADO PICK..101

CHAPTER 22: FIGHTING WITH ANDY 104

CHAPTER 23: ARE WE READY?..111

Chapter 1: Olympic Dreamer

PEDRO'S STORY

Wow, what a hot day this is, I thought, as I, Pedro Hernandez Garcia, pick up my half-full box of Chiclets gum. On Monday, Thursday, and Saturday, I head out the door to sell my wares to rushing tourists.

I don't mind the distance to the large cruise ships because I find a big stone and kick it all along the way to the docks. Twice, I was able to bounce a little rock from foot to foot for almost two blocks without it ever touching the ground. Why wasn't anyone watching?

"I am Messi, the greatest soccer player in all the world," is my daily chant.

This whole year I arrive late to school on the cruise ship days, after selling gum to help Mama get food for us. Sometimes, I have such a good day that I can buy pan dolce for my brother and sisters, Mario, Dona, and Guadalupe. They climb all over me and cheer when I able to treat them with their favorite sweet breads.

On the days there are no cruise ships in port, I can be in school all day. At recess, we get to play with a real soccer ball. The scuffed ball leaks, so we must fill it with air each time we play. The old soccer ball bounces better than a rock, so I don't complain!

On our dusty field, I take the ball anywhere, so fast, like lightning.TAP, TAP, TAP, WHISH, TRAP, then SMACK, right between our milk carton goals. I scored over and over. No one can catch me.

"Pedro never stops." I love hearing my friends say.

I learned to kick with either foot. In the beginning, my left foot seemed to have a mind of its own and wanted to send the ball well past the left edge of the field. Carlos would laugh and steal the ball as he discovered my weak spot. This made me so angry.

I started exercising my left foot and leg by placing a sock over the front of my foot. I put one rock in the toe and the other pinned in the cuff end. Night after night, I lift my leg counting to 100 twice. I kept making the rocks bigger and bigger until they could barely squeeze into their sock pockets.

Now my left leg was as strong and as my powerful right leg. I still exercise both legs whenever I read the books from our school library. I cannot seem to read anymore without one of my legs bouncing my sock rocks!

As strong as my left leg had become, it still needed better control. During spring break, I persuaded my little brother, Mario, to throw our only ball, an old tennis ball, as hard as he could towards my left foot. Little by little, I am able to trap the small ball and kick it back to Mario. I improved my kicking while Mario improved his throwing.

Just when I thought I had this yellow ball in perfect control, I tried a harder kick, only to hear a crashing sound as it broke Mama's flowerpot! The good news—it smashed only one pot. The bad news—it was our only pot in the backyard.

Hearing the noise, Mama appeared at the door. "We need to save our rose, Pedro. When you pull the thorny bush out of that half pot, and we can replant it in the corner."

I was waiting nervously to hear my punishment. Instead, I heard, "I can see that your kick is getting powerful. Be more careful, Pedro."

"Sorry, Mama," is all I could say.

I could not wait to get back to school to try my new kick with the bigger surface of a real soccer ball.

During recess the next day, I proved I was right. The school soccer ball was so much easier to direct than our puny tennis ball. I was defending my left side, making even more goals and Carlos stopped laughing.

I continued to dream of competing on a real team. How did Messi find his first team? Was it this hard?

There was always a big problem at recess. All of the players thought they were boss, so it took us half of the recess just to divide into two teams. No one wanted to be goalie, so we played without one. That is why our scores got so high in so short a time.

Last week Carlos and Marcus got in a fight, each pulling the ball his way. They both ended up on the ground, rolling over and over, still grasping the ball. It was really funny until the principal saw them and took away our ball for three days "to teach us a lesson." It just taught us to be mad at Carlos and Marcus for spoiling our fun. A real team only needs one boss, the coach.

I don't like the end of the cruise season. The big tourist crowds dwindle because the Americans are less inclined to leave their more comfortable summer temperatures in trade for the burning heat of our tropics here in Mexico.

When I get to the pier, I scoot in and out and around until I wiggle into the spot where I can easily be seen as the tourists walk into town for a day of drinking, laughing, shopping and, of course, sunbathing.

One of the main tourist attractions in our town is a bar where people hang from their feet upside down to take a drink. I could never figure out why people thought this was such a great thing to do. The few Coca-Colas I ever had, tasted most delicious when I was standing straight up!

I saw that day's tourists filled only half the seats in the small Dorey boat that brought them from the anchored ships. A larger than life man was standing up and in a booming voice said, "Do not buy Chiclets from these children. It will only encourage them to pester us." Others responded, "Yeah, yeah, yeah."

I did not understand the words, but I get the message as I have heard it before! I recognized his mean tone!

"WE ARE NOT STEALING.

WE ARE NOT BEGGING

WE ARE NOT HURTING ANYONE

WE JUST WANT YOU TO BUY OUR CHICLETS." I said.

I cannot say this in English. I can merely look with begging eyes and hope they understand.

I wish I could tell them that we just want food for our dinner. We work hard. Mama irons for the rich people. We have no Papa. Before he died, he made our home from wood and pieces of cardboard. It's small and not fancy, but we are happy. We sing and dance when Mama plays her wooden flute for us. She hugs us and makes us feel safe even when we are hungry.

"Chiclets, Chiclets, Chiclets, por favor, Chiclets." is all I could yell.

The people act as though their noses are stuck to the clouds. They like to pretend we are not there.

This was going to be a bad day for sales, I decided. I'd rather be in the schoolyard running while waiting for the bell to ring. When the cruise ships come on weekdays, I always miss the first two classes. Mrs. Rocha, my teacher, is strict but I think she understands because she writes down the page numbers that I miss.

Eventually, a bald old man tossed three pesos in my direction. I reached out, and my arm was just long enough to stop the coins from falling in the murky water. I felt like throwing the gum back to him, but customer service kicked in. I walked around and placed the purchase in his hand. A fancy woman standing beside him, wearing high-heels and an oval shaped orange hat, smiled and held up four fingers. I placed four Chiclets in her palm. She put five pesos in mine. Grabbing the brim of her hat, she tilted her head toward her thoughtless partner and added two more pesos.

I am learning that business is business. Play it smart! The other tourists headed up to the plaza, and I cannot help noticing how smug they looked at having escaped scruffy boys.

Twenty pesos today, how little food this will buy. I know Mama will smile and say that she knows I did my best, but I will be able to see the worry in her eyes.

I stopped at The Mercado after school and watched Mrs. Ramos weigh the paltry red beans in the bottom of the cone-shaped scale. They looked so meager in the shiny metal scale that dangles over the tomatoes.

"Pedro, these five bananas are too brown to sell. Would you like them?" They did not seem so brown to me, so I was excited and ran home forgetting even to kick a rock.

Two days pass. Time to meet the tourists again. I check my box and arrange the tiny gum packs in straight lines, so they look neat and tidy

Sometimes the small Dorey boats that bring passengers from the ships are delayed. As I waited, I looked to the blue ocean, and I take these moments to daydream my favorite scene. I watch myself coming to shore wearing the Olympic uniform, back from the win at Tokyo. The whole town is at the dock waving Mexican and Olympic flags to greet their hometown hero. First, our county's victory in London, now it has been my privilege to score the winning goal during my turn in Japan. They know that I am the youngest ever to be sent to the Olympics with the Mexican team! The cheering is deafening. I give them a deep and respectful bow. I see Mama's face glowing at me. This dream feels so real.

Disappointed that my favorite daydream was interrupted, I saw a group of ladies in flowered dresses and fat bellied men huffing and puffing in their Corona and Hawaiian shirts attempting to pull themselves out of the small boats. They seem to be the toughest crowd yet. The people prance by, pretending there is no one at the water's edge calling out "Chiclets, Chiclets."

My friend Emilio says, "Maybe they don't see us because they are rich and could buy all the candy they wanted until their teeth rotted out. Maybe they all have false teeth and can't even chew without losing their dentures!" We both had a good laugh from that thought.

Chapter 2: Mystery Girl

MORE PEDRO STORY

Only one sunburned couple stopped to get Chiclets. I saw the last two people getting out of the boat. It was a grey-haired smiling woman followed by a pretty girl. The girl's long blonde hair glimmered and danced in the midday sun like spun gold.

They walked along the dock laughing about some secret joke. As they came closer, I noticed that the girl is wearing a shiny white soccer ball picture on the front of her red shirt with giant letters spelling out USC. I don't know what USC means. I can't even say it. Maybe it is the name of an American team, but I didn't understand why a girl was wearing it? Grown girls do not play soccer.

Before I realized it, my brain switched from Chiclets to soccer.

I heard myself yell, "Futbol, Futbol, Futbol." instead of "Chiclets, Chiclets, Chiclets."

The girl turned to me and said, "Hola." She hesitated, making me think that may be the limit to what she possibly knew in Spanish.

Was she talking to me?

13

"Hola, Hola, Hola!" I replied.

The girl pointed to her shirt. "Soccer," she said, smiling at me.

"Si," I replied, kicking the air with a pretend ball.

The girl gave me a thumbs-up and waved for me to come up past the rocks. Forgetting about an early return to school, I followed the ladies to the sandy beach area with just five pesos jiggling in my pocket.

Bending forward, this attractive long-legged USC girl unzipped her gym bag and pulled out a gorgeous white and black shiny soccer ball. The ball was fully pumped up.

She threw the ball to me. How exciting! I knew that I could show up any girl, pretty or not. She would see.

I kicked the ball back to her. She trapped it with ease, dribbling the ball past me. As I turned, she quickly passed it back to me. I was able to trap it with my famous right foot. She ran to me and stole it back before I could blink an eye. "Wow, what just happened?"

As I hesitated, I'm sure just a second, she shot the ball between our two pieces of driftwood goals.

Again, and again she laughingly kicked it away from me, her smile expressing the fun she was having. I worked to get my groove back and scored a few times. I have the embarrassing feeling she may have let me score a few goals.

I then knew I will not put down a girl's talent without checking it out first! Who was she anyway?

I thought the other lady was her grandmother because she kept calling this enthusiastic referee 'Coach.' That must be the English name for Grandmama, I figured. This lady held her fingers up to show the score. She even took back one of my opponent's goals. I'm not sure why, but I saw the USC girl frowning at her. Coach wagged her pointer finger in her direction and shook her head.

It took one hour to tie the score at 4 to 4. When the grandma lady signaled the end of the game, I was happy that we could leave it at that. My opponent seemed to be having too much fun to stop before winning. At least I did not lose, but I was really sweaty.

As we sat on a bumpy old beach log, Mrs. Coach, as I called her, reached into her bag and pulled out a water bottle and we each squirted some into our dry mouths. She then handed me the end of her striped towel. I was not quite sure what she wanted me to do with it. What if I wiped the sweat off my face and that's not why she gave it to me? I am relieved when she took the other end and patted her face. I copied her.

This grand mama, "Coach" in English I again reminded myself, motioned me to stand up. She took the ball, bounced it in the air, and headed it to me from her grey curly head of hair. I was almost too stunned to respond. I trapped it and decided I was supposed to dribble it past her. But she stole it away before I had taken two steps. I felt like I was in the middle of a bad dream! She ran past me and shot into our pretend goal. First, a beautiful girl, and now a grand mama was showing me up!

Coach lady called me over, took a bow and laughed. I forced a smile but did not laugh.

She directed me to look at her feet and while staring in my eyes, scooped the ball with her left instep, booted it behind her and then scooped it with her right instep sending it forward with an amazing thrust. When I returned with the ball, she pointed to my feet and circled her finger to show it was my turn to make those same moves. Ten times, I tried it, improving each time.

She gave me two thumbs up. I liked my new move. I was even more like Messi now.

Except I had no team.

With a swing of her amazing hair, USC girl stood up, pointed to her mouth and rubbed her stomach.

"Hungry?" she asked, hesitating, not sure if I understood her word.

"Si," I said, hoping she was talking about food. We walked up to the small plaza where, much to my happiness, 'Coach' lady pointed to a taco stand.

Ten fish tacos and three Coca-Colas quickly appeared on the counter. How good these cold coke bubbles felt in my dry throat! So many tacos for just the three of us!

They offered me a fourth, and though I was almost full, I could not resist.

While they seemed to enjoy watching me wolf down these delicious tacos, I thought they are asking me my name.

"Pedro," I said. Yes, I was right. They were asking my name.

"Hola, Pedro," they said. The girl points to herself and says "Jacquelynn."

I never heard that name before, so I said it the best I can, three times. "Yacolynn, Yacolynn, Yacolynn." I didn't want to forget.

She smiled, then pointed to the lady next to her and says, "Coach Pia."

I nodded my head and said, "Gracias, Coach Pia," followed by my very loud burp...much louder than usual. I guess I am not used to all those bubbles. I was so embarrassed, but they just laughed so I did too. Jacquelynn pointed to both her cheeks and I think she was referring to my dimples. I was so embarrassed that I covered my eyes, and they laughed again.

As we got up from the bench, there was so much I wished I could say. USC reached into her pocket and pressed one hundred pesos into my hand. I tried to return it to her for I did not even beat her in our game!

Then the thought of Mama, happy with the food I could bring home made me close my hand around the generous gift and smile. "Gracias, Yacolynn" is all I could say. The whole family will have full stomachs. Mama's flute will sound like heaven tonight.

I tried with all my might, but I could not keep a tear from falling from my right eye and down my cheek. After two shy hugs for these kind strangers, I started up the path towards home with a happy heart.

From behind, I heard "Pedro, Pedro the Soccer Boy!"

I turned and saw Jacquelynn walking back to me. With a slight bow, she handed me that beautiful black and white soccer ball. She pointed to me and proudly gave me the "NUMBER ONE" sign with her fingers, then circled around in a victory dance before hurrying away.

It was on this day that I, Pedro Hernandez Garcia, started to believe I was truly worthy of success.

When I returned to school, I stayed after class. I asked Mrs. Rocha if she knew what the English word 'coach' was in Spanish.

"I think it is grand-mama," I explained.

"No, Pedro. In Spanish, it is entrenador, the coach who directs a sports team."

I wondered out loud how a grandmother lady could ever do that. "First, a girl player who plays better than I can play, then an older lady who is a coach! What next?"

Mrs. Rocha explained, "The USA Olympic women's soccer team had a wonderful grey-haired coach. She had the winning team. Pedro, you have a lot to learn about the modern woman."

It all seemed confusing to me. I thought girls just danced and twirled.

The next month our school got its first computer, and together with Mrs. Rocha, I found a 'Jacquelynn' on the first-string roster of the USC winning soccer team. We were also able to learn about USC and their incredible soccer fame.

That is when I fell in love with computers. Now I can know about soccer in the whole world.

I will practice harder and longer than ever with my beautiful new soccer ball.

Chapter 3: A Caterpillar Stuck in Her Cocoon

NOW ESPERANZA'S STORY

When I picture my time in Guadalajara, I remember looking down some of the streets and thinking that there was no end to the city as it seemed to go on forever. I, Esperanza Madrigal, remember the pink, orange, and red flowers that appeared to be growing everywhere, cascading over the houses, fences, and patios. They made simple houses feel rich and inviting.

Our large extended family lived in the busy city, nestled within blocks of each other. This made me feel safe and loved. Happily, my family taught me that a soccer match must be a part of our family celebrations, large or small. At first, my only job was to run after the ball if it bounced into the garden area at Grand Mamas. They felt little feet were less likely to trample her favorite plants.

I felt it was unfair that I could not play on one of our family teams. After all, I was already 10 years old. I'm sure I whined to Papa in excess. I can remember the very moment he told me he would start my real training so I could join our games.

He smiled and said, "I must get you ready now. We cannot let you embarrass the Francisco Madrigal name, the finest name in all of Mexico."

Though he acted as if he were kidding, part of him must have been serious because, after that, he rarely missed a day bringing the ball out for our practice as soon as he got home from work. Believe me, his practices were hard work, but they were the most fun too.

He decided to put me in a weekly gymnastics class. He assured me that training my leg-eye coordination, along with developing my leg and foot muscles, would give me a keen sense of balance and power that would help in soccer. I wasn't sure about all that, but soon I began to feel a real difference in my body muscles. That's when I became willing to increase my weekly lesson to twice a week. The beam was my favorite event, and I'll never forget my first backflip on it. I was amazed that the beam as right there to grab. Gave me confidence. As the only gym for many miles around, we could only compete among ourselves, but we liked to imagine we could beat anyone.

"My training will make you as good as any boy." Papa would say.

"How about better than any boy?" was my quick retort.

"But never better than your old man," he replied with a wink.

Four months later, my cousin Oscar received his Confirmation at the Assumption of Our Lady Cathedral. It was a big deal because he was able to choose his own middle name, something to do with becoming a man. He chose his uncle's name, Francisco, which made my Papa stand tall and proud.

The Confirmation seemed long, with music, prayers, the bishop gently slapping each teen's cheeks, and then more prayers. When it was over, the hungry relatives gathered at our house so Papa could give his godson a big celebration. I hurried through the delicious meal of enchiladas, chili rellenos and, my favorite, flan. I wanted to be ready for the soccer game.

I was excited because it was my time to start playing with the family. No more just retrieving the ball from the garden.

Dinner finished, tables cleared and folded, there was finally room in the courtyard to play our game. I stood proudly in the center. This is where we would choose teams.

"You'd better move out of the way, little one."

"I am playing today, Uncle Ernesto."

"What, of course, you are not! You are a girl, and you are too little.

I glared as hard as I could and remember stamping my foot at him. I pulled the ball to me, and as I maneuvered away from him, said, "Come get the ball away, Uncle."

He chased me from one end of the large yard to the other and could not steal the ball away. Some of it was talent, a bit of it was luck. My heart was beating fast as I was determined to earn a spot on my family's roster. I continued to glare as I felt it made me look less girly.

Clapping erupted from the sidelines after I kicked the ball into our homemade goal. Point made, or so I hoped.

Grand mama appeared in the doorway. "Esperanza, what do you think you are doing, Mija? Soccer is a boy's game. Come sit by me and watch like a good girl."

"This feisty one just earned the right play a game," Uncle Ernesto said, shaking his head. I stayed on the field right behind Uncle.

Papa was enjoying the drama but remained quiet. He had told me part of my training was learning to stand up for myself. I guess this was one of those times. He liked to call me his little warrior. I heard it even though his face was silent.

Our courtyard was not as big as a real field, but it did give me a chance to run, with the ball of course. Papa was on my team, a deadly combo. Kick, pass, kick and pass. All those hours taught me just how he thinks and moves. Like clockwork... this became the best day of my life. That was the day I first heard my nickname, 'Super Es.' I loved it, and it became music to my ears, or so I thought until Ernesto called for a break.

I looked up and saw all the aunts and grandmothers gathered on the porch. I kept looking away. I did not intend to make myself noticed by the ladies, who had expressed worry about my lack of ladylikeness in the past.

Ignoring them was apparently not going to work as their conversation seemed to get louder and their hands were flying in all directions as they spoke.

Oh, Pain! I heard Auntie Julia calling my name. Pretended not to hear her, then I heard my grand mama calling my name, and I knew it was time to face the firing squad. I walked over to the shady veranda looking as tall and grown as my short frame would let me. Their silent raised eyebrows were flags of trouble.

"Anyone want me to get them the flan for dessert?" I said, trying distraction at this point.

"No, young lady." was the stern reply of all five of them in unison.

"You sound like a choir," I replied.

Silence filled the air. I saw where humor was not going to soften the day, either.

"Sit, Esperanza," the women said. "We know you do not have a mama to guide you. We feel that you are not learning the right rules about life. Your mama named you Esperanza Vita Louise Madrigal. As you know, Esperanza Vita means hope for life. Hope for your life and for her life. She would rock you and sing to you every day. She would say, 'My baby is special. A perfect life is my hope for her. It will be bigger and better than mine.'"

"Your Mama Carmelita had been sick for two years and never expected to be able to have you, so you were her miracle, Mija. She was able to shower love on her little baby for the year before she died. We wish she could have been with you long enough for you to remember her. We promised her we would guide you in the ways of a woman."

"But I do remember how Mama smelled. When I smell roses, I know she is close," I whispered.

The aunts looked surprised. "Yes, we had forgotten. That is the perfume she always wore. How did you know?"

"I have always known."

"Esperanza," Aunt Julia stood up, "we want you to give up playing soccer. It is not a girl's game. You will get hurt. Boys will not think of you as pretty. They will not want you for a wife. We want you to go to dance class with our daughters instead. We will take you every Wednesday. You are pretty. Boys will love to watch you dance. Your life will be good."

It made me feel like my life was over. Why do I have to be just like everyone else? Will my Mama be disappointed in her hope? Will she stop letting me smell her roses if I do not please her?

My mood felt as dark as the storm clouds that were forming over our city. After everyone left, I hurried under my covers, curled up, and listened to the sky roar and cry its volume of tears.

"Sky, I know just how you feel."

Chapter 4: Time for a Change

STILL ESPERANZA'S STORY

Gratefully, I awoke the next day to sunshine. Papa must have not heard the lecture last night because he walked into my tiny room with his favorite soccer ball tucked under his arm.

"Training starts in 15 minutes," he announced. "I was proud of how well you kept possession of the ball yesterday. Your header into the right upper corner was dead on, dear one."

Obviously, he did not get the memo about me stopping soccer.

"We are going to the wall today," said Papa.

"What wall? Why are we going there?"

"There is a tall brick wall at the Presidente Park. It'll teach you to kick faster as the ball bounces back so quickly. It is how I taught my legs to score without thinking. And you will too if you try every day, Esperanza."

Right after breakfast, we hurried the three blocks to the park. Papa knew this was a perfect wall for kicking and rebounding.

It quickly turned out to be harder than it looks. That ball seemed to come back to me faster than corn popping. Each day it got easier, missing the ball less and less often. I think that gymnastics practice helped me learn to balance when I needed to change feet. Thank you, beam!

The next week I proudly showed my father how I had progressed with the ball and wouldn't you know it, he gave me a new task! Now he wanted me to kick at least one-half the attempts with just my instep! He definitely did not get the memo. Now he thinks he is an Olympic trainer!

I pretended to be overworked, but it was actually fun to work hard and get better. I want to have lightning fast passes, just like my father.

My third instep kick landed me smack on my rear! Guess you could say my kick was a bit too high! Rubbing my butt, I quickly looked around to see who might be watching. There was my friend Gilbert laughing his head off. That was bad enough, but when he added "Girly, girl" to his laughter, I ran after him. It was a good thing I was slowed by my pain you know where, otherwise he would have been mine.

Papa is an x-ray technician. He worked at San Javier hospital in the radiology department. That is where they take pictures of your bones and liver and even your brain. He worked early in the morning but was home by 4:00 o'clock, unless he was on call, so we were able to spend a lot of time together each day.

Three months after the Confirmation he told me that he got a promotion and that he had good news and bad news. I figured it was time to sit down so I could take it all in.

He started with the good news. He would be in charge of his own department in a new hospital with new equipment. He was also happy that he would be making more money.

The bad news came next. The hospital was three hours away in a small town by the ocean. We will have to move and make new friends. We will still be able to come back and see our relatives but not as often as now.

"Oh," I thought. "Maybe this is not such bad news after all."

I would miss my relatives, but there would be no grannies or aunties close by to make me forget soccer and replace it with a dumb dance class.

"Could I play soccer there?" I ask.

"We will have to see, Esperanza," Papa replied.

Chapter 5: Rise of the Panthers

BACK TO PEDRO'S STORY

"A real soccer ball," I say over and over.

I, Pedro, had never even seen a new soccer ball in person. And now it was mine. I ran home to share my good fortune, but I was so out of breath, I could hardly speak. When I finally managed to get the story out, Mario, Dona, Luis and Guadalupe each needed to check out the bounce of this crisp black and white ball.

It hit every corner of our tiny home, but no one cared how much it disheveled the piles of folded clothes and blankets. Mama brought out her flute and played while we all danced with our new possession. Because of the money I received today, our tummies were full on this lucky June night, and we all fell asleep, feeling very rich.

When the new school year started, I continued to use the old scuffed ball at recess even though it needed pumping up with air each day. No way was I ready to share my good ball and let everyone kick it.

That October, a serious looking muscular man came to my school. Mrs. Rocha said he was to meet with the boys. The rumor was that he was there to announce more math classes. We filed into an open area by the side door. As the man walked near us, he looked into our eyes and announced that we were to run around the border of the school's dry, dusty field.

We wondered what that had to do with the time's tables? Maybe he thinks if our bodies are tired, we can pay better attention.

Carlos refused to run, saying he only will run for soccer. Marcos agreed, saying that he did not know who this new man was but was sure he was not his boss.

The man stood up and took out a blue notebook after sending Carlos and Marcos back to their class. He watched us. We were all glad to run around the field for any reason. It's always better than sitting still at our desks.

"Who likes soccer?" asks the man. "Who is willing to work hard?"

Many of us were wondering what these questions had to do with math. We were puzzled.

"My name is Alejandro Vargas, but you can call me Coach. There is a new soccer league starting in town, and we are forming three teams so far. I am here to recruit players who want to win and are willing to work hard. We will be practicing after school three times a week. You boys are the luckiest ones because you have the best coach, me. I will train you to be the best too. That is why I have named the team The Panthers, for their sleek beauty and agility but mostly for their speed. You will learn to be fast. I will show you how, but you will have to show me that you are willing to work hard because I am not willing to settle for less than your best. When you go home today, talk to your parents. Sign-ups will be tomorrow."

We could hardly believe our ears. Real soccer for us was such a distant dream. We had only seen the pro teams through the windows of the Amigos Bar in town. There were so many of us trying to get a peek at the TV that it was a push and shove contest just to get a glimpse. Regardless, we were always there on game day because the yelling, screaming and punching each other was so much fun, interrupting our otherwise dull life.

"You're dismissed," says the curly headed man. "Back to your class and tell those two stubborn ones to come back if they are ready to listen."

Our whole group hurried away chattering loudly. A few minutes later, Carlos and Marcos returned with their eyes to the ground.

Carlos and Marcos told us at lunch what happened when they returned to the field.

They said the man named Alejandro told them, "I know you didn't realize who I was when I asked you to run. That is why I am willing to give you another chance to be on my soccer team."

The boys' eyes brightened as they told us. When we had announced there would be a soccer team, they felt they had blown their chances.

The man then said to them, "I am glad to see you thinking for yourselves, but if you want to join us you need to know that as a coach, I will expect constant obedience to my directives. I am here to win. Are you ready to give it your all?"

Marcos agreed at once, as soccer was his family's life. Marcos turned to Carlos and noted his hesitation. He said, "We all know about your stubbornness, Carlos. Obedience has not been your best quality. Just because you're big, doesn't mean you can always be boss of everything. Your skills do not match that big ego yet."

Later, gathered around classmates, Carlos boasted "I think the Panthers would be lucky to have us. The Coach even said our size is an advantage, and that may make us good back fielders. Coach also said time would tell. I think he'll be lucky to have us blocking the ball."

34

We all shook our heads at Carlos, our loudest big mouth.

Our teachers found it particularly hard to keep their classes in proper order for the rest of the day. We squirmed like jumping beans.

Meanwhile, Coach could not wait to start. This was his chance to show people who he really was.

When I returned home, I told Mama about the new team. "I know how happy Papa will be to know that I, Pedro, am going to be on a real soccer team!" Mama gave me an extra long hug. "I am sure he will be looking down proudly at every game and be cheering the loudest," she said as tears rimmed her eyes.

That night when I was lying on our large mattress along with my brother and baby sisters, I prayed to my father to help me make my left foot as strong and accurate as my right. I figure after this long year, my Papa must, by now, know everything and everyone in heaven, and have the best influence with all those saints who do miracles.

The next afternoon, Alejandro was on the dusty school field taking sign-ups in that blue notebook. He was surrounded by eager participants. I, Pedro Hernandez Garcia, was more than ready. I felt like I was born ready.

"Practice will begin tomorrow afternoon, down at the beach at 3:00 o'clock. Be sure and let your parents know where you will be."

We saw the coach walk to his car and sit inside, not turning the key just yet. Was he thinking or just remembering?

Chapter 6: A Checkered Past

ALEJANDRO'S COACH STORY

Coach Alejandro was very excited to have a chance for a team of his own. During and after high school he was a star player on his way to an outstanding soccer career. As a boy, Alejandro Vargas also lived in Guadalajara, a bustling city, where the Blessed Virgin Mary and soccer are both adored. Often Mary, mother of Jesus, was implored to intervene, especially for one of the Mexican National teams. Everyone believes this is a proper prayer, but no one actually knows whether she even understands the rules of futbol.

Alejandro, the youngest son in the Vargas family, was on a futbol team ever since the age of seven and by high school had become a soccer legend. Coaches vied to get him on their team. Everyone knew he would be invited to play on one of the National Teams after graduation. He was the top scorer, and the newspapers loved to feature their favorite son.

His older brother Beto was on the Mexican National Team when he lost his leg to cancer. Alejandro was not only aspiring to a career for himself but to honor the brother who was his hero. The newspaper had announced that the newest Vargas would be Guadalajara's and probably Mexico's greatest player ever. People gathered around him wherever Alejandro went.

Fate is not always kind.

One sultry Saturday night he and his friends were out celebrating Mexico's win over Chile. Hector, the driver, stopped at a liquor store saying that he could get them a real celebration. Next thing they heard was the sound of gunfire, and then they saw Hector running back to the car with a look of terror on his face and a gun in his hand. He sped away with his two bewildered passengers in the car. In what seemed like a split second, the sound of a siren followed their speeding auto.

The rest is history as Alejandro, and his friend spent the next three years behind bars. The driver got life for killing the clerk even though he insisted the gun had accidentally fired.

The city was aghast. The papers went crazy. Sports editors turned their backs on Alejandro. How could their hopes and dreams vanish so quickly? Alejandro simply became a memory.

He then sat in a dinky cell, which not only imprisoned his body, but also his dream. His perfectly toned body became diminished by the 10x12 foot space. Running in place helped control his anger, but his knuckles often were scabbed from punching the wall late at night. Over the last year, Skinner Johansen, a tattooed blonde man from California who thought drug smuggling might make him rich, occupied the cell with him. Alejandro worked hard at learning English, giving him a sense of accomplishment.

"Hey, Dude," Skinner reminded him. "I don't know no proper English, but it will do for a start." Alejandro taught Skinner to box as he figured that was a most useful skill for this kind of thinker.

The days moved slowly. As soon as he was released, he went to live with Uncle Santos and work on his avocado ranch near the coast. Uncle Santos was glad to have his favorite nephew's help with the trees. Even more, he felt lucky to have help speaking English during negotiations with American grocery outlets. Alejandro felt grateful to have a new start far away from the shame.

Soccer was still in his heart and the single most important thing he cared about now. When he learned a youth soccer league was starting, he felt that it would break up the monotony of laboring in the quiet avocado orchards. A way to be part of the game, to win again, and this time he had to win. The fire within started to burn again. No looking back.

Chapter 7: And What a Change!

ESPERANZA AGAIN

The next two weeks were filled with making plans, packing, and saying goodbye. I was happy and scared all at once.

The new town seemed so little and so poor. Tiny shops, tiny streets, so few cars. People did not dress fancy. Everything seemed plain. I was used to living in the middle of gardens of flowers. There were no gyms for training or even a movie theater. It felt like the Grinch had come to town.

The only hospital was new but looked miniature compared to the ones in Guadalajara. The town did not even have buses! Can you imagine that?

In two days, we found a house to live in. I had always wanted to live in a pink house and was disappointed to see it was brown, and a puke-brown at that. The inside was bright and cozy. My room was big enough for all my things and I stayed up late arranging everything just so. There were even shelves in my closet where I lined up my treasures.

As I awoke late in the morning, I heard a ladder sliding against the outside wall. There was Papa with a paint can in one hand and a brush in the other.

"Surprise! I know you always wanted to live in a pink house. I want you to live in a pink house, Esperanza. The owner said I could paint it. Want to help?"

"I love pink!"

"I know!" Papa chuckled.

I changed out of my pajamas as quickly as I could, drank some orange juice, grabbed a pan dulce, stuffed it into my mouth, ran outside and dipped my brush into the creamiest prettiest pink paint ever. I began brushing pink and more pink and even pinker, everywhere I could reach. This was my most pink ever, and I did not want to stop. So much of me became pink that Papa took the hose to me when we finished!

He laughed at my dripping self and said, "Next week we will plant flowers. How about pink bougainvilleas? That way everyone can find us!"

"Roses too, Papa."

A week later, I watched my Mr. Francisco Madrigal bring home a huge piece of cardboard. Papa had retrieved it from a large box that brought the X-ray machine to his department.

"Whatever Is that for?" I asked.

"It is your header board, Mija."

"My bed already has a headboard."

"No, no, a soccer headboard. Come to the back, and I will show you. Games are often won by the teams that can do the best headers. The ball is going to come to your head often anyway, but it is how you use your head to direct it into the goal that will make the difference. This exercise will help build your neck muscles so your neck bones will be protected while giving direction to the ball.

He got out his knife and started cutting a hole in the center.

"No, no, you are making it too little, Silly Father," I protested.

He stepped back and saw that it was just a little bigger than the ball.

"I think you have a point." He poked his own head in, and it got stuck.

"Now you are the one with the point," I teased as he widened the circle.

He was right. It definitely takes practice to get direction on the ball. For obvious reasons, we decided to start with one of our softer beach balls. It actually became more comfortable as I improved with practice.

We were pleased to see we had a windowless wall next to the back door of our wonderful pink house. We did not have to go to a park for that part of the practice anymore. Once it was determined that the paint was good and dry, I would kick, kick, kick the ball to my own wall and back. Papa will probably have to paint over the scuff marks a time or two.

School days were looming. I never had to change schools before. It can be frightening. Will I be behind in class work? Will I look stupid? Will I have friends? Will they like sports? I found myself hoping for a stomachache, flu, or heck I'd even give up my appendix just to be able to stay home a little longer. No such luck. Monday was drawing near.

Uniforms there are white shirts and blue pants or skirt. Easy peasy! I like fashion that I don't have to think about in the morning. I, of course, chose pants.

Papa brought me to the office where we met the principal. I was surprised at how tiny and old the building seemed. The principal showed me a list of rules, but all I really wanted to know was what time recess was. On the way to my new classroom, I remained silent while Ms. Ortega pointed out the recess yard. What the heck! It was a lumpy dirt field, with spurts of grass that looked like an old man who was losing his hair. I was missing my old school with its manicured field already. No swings or monkey bars? Guess not.

I again wished I could run all the way back to my pretty, pink house!

Ms. Rocha, my new teacher, was nice. After introducing me to the other students, she gave me a seat up front. My desk was very wobbly with initials carved all over its wooden surface, which made my writing bumpy. It made me feel even more nervous, so I kept my head looking down most of the morning.

Finally recess! The girls walked to the end of the field, sat and started chatting. Oh dear, is this recess?

The boys were playing dodge ball. No one looked at me.

I decided to run, as I figured this would make me feel more relaxed. I ran across the field one, two times, then all the way around five more times.

Recess was over when the bell clanged. One of the girls said, "You really run fast," as we filed back into class. "You don't run at all." Only my mind responded.

I brought my lunch, but by now I was so nervous my stomach wanted to do flip-flops rather than be hungry. We ate at two tables in the back of our room. Not like my old, real cafeteria, but at least some of the girls talked to me.

That afternoon the boys were called out to the field for a meeting and returned all excited. They said a coach came to tell them that there were three soccer teams forming in town and one was going to be chosen from the boys at this school.

Signups would be tomorrow. The boys were given papers to take home to their parents.

Chapter 8: Rejection is Ugly

ESPERANZA SPEAKING

After class, I asked Mrs. Rocha if I could have papers.

"Are you asking to play? Esperanza?"

"I have always wanted to play on a real team."

"No, I'm afraid it is just for the boys. Girls don't play on soccer teams. We have Girl Scouts every other Thursday right here after school. I think you would enjoy that more."

I could not wait to get back to the safety of my little pink house.

Would I ever fit in?

The next day I watched as the new coach was signing up the boys. He was tall and muscular and looked so intense that I dared not interrupt him. Actually, I was in no mood to be refused.

"We will be practicing down at the beach starting tomorrow," the man named Alejandro Vargas announced.

I realized that the beach he was talking about is just blocks from my beautiful pink house.

On the first day of practice, I left a note for Papa, grabbed my ball and ran to the beach as the soon-to-be team arrived. I dribbled the ball again and again to the water and back. It felt good to be on the beach. I love to feel the warm sand sift through my toes. The beach is my happy place, so soccer dribbling does not seem like work. Yet no one seemed to notice me.

The boys were mostly running drills on the first day. I was glad to see that only two boys, a Pedro, and a Juan, were fast. I knew I could beat the others running backward. Pedro and Juan, however, would be a challenge. I felt confident that I was ready for them. Bring it on.

I continued to run. I can see where this team will need me, and I will be ready for these butt nuggets!

Practice finished. I was glad to see Papa as I spotted pink just as I turned our corner. He looked up with a shovel in his hands.

"I thought we could celebrate your second school day by planting a bougainvillea right by our front door. That way it will welcome you each day as you return.

"Is it pink?"

"Right now, it is green, but soon it will be bursting with pink. You silly goose, do you think I would buy any other color for my best girl? Next month we will shop for roses."

"Tell me about your day at school."

"It was ok, not at all like a big city school." I went on to describe my day in detail. Papa perked up when I told him about practicing next to the soccer team.

"It is only for boys, Papa. Mrs. Rocha would not give me a soccer sign-up paper yesterday, and no one talked to me today at practice. Papa, I know I am ready to play."

Papa was quiet after that. Sometimes it is hard for a parent to know what to say. As he kissed me good night, he said, "Pray to your Mama for patience. She will hear you."

Chapter 9: Playing By Myself

MORE ESPERANZA

I am glad Pedro sits next to me in class. The next morning, he said, "How did you learn to run so fast?"

"I just like to run. I like to play soccer too."

A girl named Mia Elena shared her lunch with me. Her shiny black hair went all the way down to her waist, and her eyes had an amazing tint of green mixed into the brown that made them twinkle. She told me about her big family and that they all play music. As we traded snacks, I hoped she would be my special friend.

After school, I returned to my beach with my ball. Today I set up pieces of driftwood that I would kick the ball around. Maybe the coach would be impressed with my ball control, not just my speed.

I was trying to get up my nerve to talk to him. He did not even seem to notice my footwork that I considered awesome. At the end of practice, I said to myself, "This is it, 'Scaredy Pants'! You are wasting time. Nothing will happen as long as you stand back wishing."

Coach was standing next to Pedro.

"Coach, may I ask you something?"

"Sure."

"I've played soccer since I was five. I am pretty good. I want to play on your team."

Coach Alejandro looked down at me and frowned while shaking his head. "You are a girl, Mija, and a pretty one at that. Girls do not play soccer. I do not have room for a girl on my team. You would get hurt. I think you need to learn to dance."

Not again. That is all I hear! His affectionate term, Mija, did not lessen the blow.

As I walked away, I heard Pedro say, "Coach, I once met an older girl who played better than any boy I ever played with or even saw play."

"Pedro, you must be dreaming. No more talk of that." Alejandro walked away, still shaking his dumb head.

I get so mad when I don't get a chance at things. This was quite the predicament. I was in a dumb town, in a dumb school and now this dumb coach. I kicked sand all down the beach toward home so that it flew all the way up to my shoulder. I was pretending that it was sand-fairy dust, and it could turn me into a boy if I could stir it up enough. Was I ever mad at the world!

Luckily, I was still a girl as I reached my beautiful pink house. The color seemed to calm me a little. I said "hello" to my bougainvillea growing against the arch. I heard that if you talk to your plants, they will grow faster and not get sick. Today I was glad plants don't talk back.

It took a long time to tell Papa the reason for my grouchy mood. After all, he is a guy. How could he understand? Besides, I didn't want to talk about it at all. I just need to be mad for a while, so I decided to lie on my bed and listen to the radio. Music is calming for me.

I didn't get up until dinner and only got up when I found out we were having cheese enchiladas. I think Papa was trying his best to make up for this dumb move we made. Lucky for me, he is as good a cook as anyone's mama.

The delicious, gooey, chewy enchilada brightened my mood a bit. My practice had made me hungrier than I realized. "Yes, I'll have another, please."

"What is making my Esperanza sad?"

"I asked today if I could join the new soccer team, and they said no because I am a girl. They could see I am fast and can control the ball if only they would notice me. Coach said I would get hurt."

"They have no idea how tough you are."

"I will keep going because I like running on the beach. The sand makes my feet and legs stronger."

"I bet you could outrace any of those boys, my graceful thoroughbred," Papa responded "I was concerned when you were in bed earlier as there is a bad flu going around. We were very busy at the hospital with many extra sick people. Get your rest and wash your hands often so you can stay well."

Chapter 10: Not a girl!

BACK TO PEDRO'S STORY

Thursday afternoon, we twelve boys eagerly arrived at the beach. Coach was sitting on a soccer ball with a big water jug close by, holding his blue notebook and a big roll of duct tape.

Practice started with a coach lecture. "I know you usually play on the field, but first I am going to show you how to be the fastest runners. Sand builds both your feet and leg muscles. After playing on the beach, the field will seem easy.

You all love soccer, but since this is your first time on a team, you have a lot to learn. There is nothing more important than realizing there are no stars on this team. No hot shots that are determined to carry the ball all the way down the field and shoot the ball into the goal. It's teamwork that makes you win, time after time.

It's all about each of you knowing where your teammates are on the field. That is why I will always be reminding you to come back to your position. When you know your assigned positions and don't wander off, the rest of the team can count on where you will be. This is part of what will make us winners. Remember this. There are only two positions; on the field and off the field. When on the field, your job is to be there for your friends at all times. Be there! You will hear me say that over and over until it sings in your brains."

Alejandro then instructed the first two runs for the boys were to be in the deep sand. The last three runs were up and down the wet, firmer area bordering the ocean.

"Why does he make us go so far, Pedro?" asks Juan.

"Don't ask," I replied. "Just do it!"

Upon completion of our first runs, Coach then loosely duct taped our bare forefeet with the silver duct tape for stability when kicking the ball. Game on! Shirtless verses shirts. Driftwood goals, hot sun, elbows pushing, feet tripping, sweat rolling...interrupted only by Coach's whistle.

"Ok, ok, gather round." As the boys passed the water bottle, Coach looked at each one of us, in what seemed like too much silence.

"You are a scruffy team right now. Looks like your best virtue is speed, and I've shown you how we will increase that. You are tough, but that can get you too many penalties, which can lose a game. Since we are not losers, I will show you how to have Panther like slick qualities, so your opponents will not know what hit them. It takes practice, men."

We played until the sun went down over the waves.

"I have here papers for you to study. There will be a test on soccer rules with three questions at the beginning of each practice," says Coach. "Each wrong answer will merit 20 push-ups. Are you with me?"

My sweaty head was buzzing. "Now I know for sure I can be as good as Pele."

Marcos was frowning. "I never want to do 20 push-ups for a wrong answer. Time to study up."

Carlos simply scowled.

Next day at recess, I made the boys play soccer. "No more dodge ball," I say, "because that won't help us. Besides, it's much easier to go fast on these weeds than on the sand."

During the second practice at the beach, two more boys joined the team. Oddly enough, I noticed the new girl in our class who seemed to be tagging along with a soccer ball in her hands. While we Panthers practiced, she was a short distance away separated by a giant limb of ancient driftwood. She kicked her ball from foot to foot with ease. She repeatedly ran to the end of the beach and back, kicking her ball with scarcely a notice from anyone.

After practice, I watched her walk up to Alejandro Vargas. "My name is Esperanza. I want to play. Could I try out for the team?"

Coach looked at her as if she were loco. "No, of course not! It's a boys' game. There are no girls on other teams. No, of course not."

I stood next to the coach. After she walked away with her head hanging down, I said in my quietest voice "Excuse me, Coach, I once met a white girl who was a better player than any boy I ever saw. She is really fast. Have you seen what moves she does with the ball?"

"Sorry Pedro but the rules are the rules. Girls would just hold us back."

Esperanza Louise Madrigal kept showing up on the beach. At school, she would run next to us when we would race at recess and usually came in right behind Juan and me. But, in truth, she was not nearly as winded.

There she was again at practice, kicking the ball by herself over the sand along the blue waves of the sea and back. She would maneuver the ball around the smaller pieces of driftwood with ease. I wondered why she did not get bored.

Our team was improving. "We'll soon be practicing on a real field," says Coach.

We all noticed how much stronger our legs felt now since we had started playing on that darn sand. Juan and I were scoring frequently as we practiced in the forward position, learning to use both our left and right feet more equally than ever before. Coach said he was hoping one of the other boys would get up to speed to complete the front line, but that hadn't happened yet. He would keep pushing for the best front line, running us backward, sideways…with and without the ball.

"A good team knows that when you have the ball, you need to be playing offense. All of you," says Coach. "When the other team has the ball, you are all on defense. That is what you need to believe and carry out. That will give us momentum."

We listened and began to believe.

At the end of practice, he asked, "Do each of you have a black shirt? If not, try to find one to borrow. I want my black Panthers to be ready for our first game."

"I have a black shirt with 'Pepsi' on the front," says Philippe.

"Fine, just wear it inside out," was Coach's answer.

Coach then asked, "Who has shoes?" Flip-flops seemed to be the answer of the day.

"Maybe we will be called the Floppers," joked Manuel.

Smiling, Alejandro said, "Looks like there is work to be done here. The first game will probably be in two weeks."

The flu had overtaken the town. It seemed everyone was sick. School attendance was sparse. Only nine boys showed up for this first day of field practice. Four on one scrimmage team and five on the other. Coach was frustrated. "Maybe today, you could let Esperanza play to make the teams even," I suggested to the coach.

"OK, just for today. This is going to be a bad practice day anyway. I will put her on the weak side, so she won't hurt your and Juan's chances of scoring."

Coach blew his whistle. Esperanza controlled the ball and dribbled it through Juan and me to score a goal. Coach was angry. "Why did you let the girl through?"

We did not want to admit to Coach that we did not let her through. By the end of practice, Coach reluctantly concluded that it was her skill that repeatedly got her through. She seemed to balance on one leg as easily as two. Her headers were direct and amazingly accurate.

After practice, Coach called her over. "How did you learn such headers?" he asked.

"Papa loves futbol," replies Esperanza. "He says the secret is good headers. Papa made a hole in a big piece of cardboard. He throws the ball, and my job is to head it through the hole. I have been doing it every day. Pretty good, huh? Maybe your team should do it too."

Coach was in thought mode. He reached in his bag and pulled out the rulebook. What a front line I would have if Esperanza could be one of the forwards.

Over and over, he turned pages as our team sat silently waiting.

Finally, Alejandro spoke. "There is nothing I can see in the rulebook that says no girls. It refers to the boys, but nowhere does it say no girls allowed. Can you come tomorrow, Esperanza?"

I saw her beaming smile in response.

It appeared as if Coach's heartbeat speeded up. As he jumped over the ball, his feet seemed to be clapping. The first game was two weeks away. No matter what team he was on, we knew Coach Vargas did not like to lose. This was his first team as a coach, and he told us he was determined to start with a win. He now had his front line strong.

Chapter 11: Finally!

ESPERANZA'S STORY AGAIN

The next day, Coach gathered his team around him, took a deep breath, and asked who here was in for being the best and never looking back. Shouts of jubilance greeted his question. I do believe I was the loudest. He then asked, "Are you willing to work harder than ever?"

"Si" was the answer, all around. I was sitting at the edge of the group. When Coach introduced me as their new player, he was met with some frowns.

Marcos shook his head.

Carlos spit on the ground, "I don't want a girl on my team."

"Stop right there with your attitude! Stand up, Carlos! Come with Esperanza to this starting line. I will be at the finish line. Whoever gets there last has to run the distance five more times. Agreed?"

Carlos answered with a thumbs up and a big smile. We merely nodded as we walked, "Yes." I tried not to show my delight with the challenge.

Coach went down the field, way past the practice area. "Go!"

I allowed him to be head-to-head through the halfway point when my swinging ponytail pulled away like the determined racehorse I am and beat the panting big fullback by yards. I enjoyed the clapping from my new team as the loser began to pay his debt.

Alejandro quickly announced, "Come to me if anyone has a problem deciding who they want to work with. We are the Panthers, and I am your coach. Now the rest of you, get off your rears and start playing."

Right on, Coach!

And, play we did. Over, around, back and forth...we continued to work the ball. We were now able to have more ball time because we could also use my ball.

Chapter 12: Headers Made Happy

PEDRO'S SPEAKING AGAIN

Coach announced that he had just received the schedule and the game in two weeks would start at 9 o'clock on Saturday morning.

My heart fell. On Saturdays, I sell Chiclets to the people getting off the cruise ships at the dock. I cannot afford to miss a workday. Mama needs the money. I had so hoped the game would not start until 10 o'clock when I would be finished.

I would need to tell Coach, but not today. I know the team was counting on me to win, but I couldn't seem to find the courage to disappoint Coach, or myself.

At the start of the next practice, only Antonio missed a soccer rule answer, and his face was red even before he started his pushups.

A well-muscled man with a thick black mustache accompanied Esperanza. The man and Coach stepped aside in quiet conversation while our team did routine stretches.

The sun beat down while the ball flew back and forth down the field. Each of us continued to learn our position while still concentrating on making our legs strong and agile.

Finally, our team was instructed to take a water break. Coach and muscle man nodded to each other and took the field. Their footwork was amazing. Our team looked on with open mouths. Will we ever be that good?

Esperanza yelled, "Do another header, Papa." The boys all looked surprised. Papa obliged and then turned and winked at his daughter.

The team went back to practice with the energy of Panthers. Soon they would also have the smooth moves of one. I was the happiest I had ever been, and my kicks between the goals became more and more accurate. I knew I could help the team win. Confidence was a new but welcome attitude.

"I will tell the coach tomorrow that I can't make the first half of the first game. I think I can make it by halftime. Today has been too good, and I don't want to ruin a good thing," I heard myself mumble as I headed for home. Besides, I still had not figured out how to disappoint Coach.

Next practice, we watched Francisco, Esperanza's father, carry a well-worn giant piece of brown cardboard with a hole in the center onto the field.

After warming up, Coach explained to the boys that being good at headers will often be the difference between a good team and a great team.

The two men held up the large target as we took turns attempting to score with our heads. When the hole began to fray, Coach pulled out his trusty duct tape to reinforce it. Soon most of us better understood how to aim the ball accurately, as it bounced off different sections of our heads. Watching how this new girl maneuvered her shots gave us lessons we never expected.

Only three boys and Esperanza reported that they had real shoes. As the team scrimmaged, Francisco directed while Coach called his striker, Antonio, over and sat him on a boulder. Out came the silvery duct tape.

"Let me try something Mejo," as he lifted Antonio's leg to his lap. Keeping the flip flop on, he rolled the taped inside out so it would not stick to his skin, around and around the rubber thong, over and over the ankle and under the sole and then on top, sticky side to sticky side.

"What?" exclaimed Antonio.

"Those are your 'Duct' shoes. The rulebook says you must play with shoes. Now get out there and run as fast as you can. You are our tester."

His footwear lasted all practice and then some. Alejandro did learn that he was going to have to put holes in the tape so the sweat could get out. They weren't Nikes, but they would certainly qualify in the rulebook.

I considered telling Coach about the Saturday problem but convinced myself that it could wait until next week's practice. I could not get past the knot in my stomach! This knot was even greater than the hunger I have often felt.

This weekend Mama was lucky as she got extra ironing jobs. She was able to find a black shirt at the flea market that was only a little too big. She was so excited to give it to me in time for the first game. "Nothing this important has happened in a very long time, Pedro."

Monday's practice went well. We found out the other new team we were to play Saturday had named themselves The Iguanas. They started their practices one month before our Panthers.

"Too bad," says Coach. "But we will catch up. I notice that each of you seems to come to a stop when there are two or more players on you. Always remember that when there are two or three opponents on you, more of your teammates will be in the open, unguarded. Best time to pass. If you see that happening, you will get the ball past them more times than not. Cherish those opportunities."

Alejandro then set up three two-on-one drills. I started finding more holes to pass through. The others also saw more opportunities and confidence soared.

Francisco brought three pairs of old shoes and gave them to three happy boys. The coach reinforced the loose soles on two of them with his favorite sticky tool.

At the end of Thursday's practice, I finally found the courage to ask the coach if I could talk to him. "What's up, Bro?"

Hesitating, not knowing where to begin. "I...I...uh, I will not be at the start of the game this Saturday, Coach."

"Why not?"

"I work early on Saturdays at the dock selling Chiclets to the people getting off the cruise ships. I don't get done until 9:30 at the earliest, Coach, but I will run to the field as soon as I am done."

"Why did you not tell me this sooner, Pedro?"

"I was afraid to disappoint you."

"I want you to respect me, Mejo, but I do not want you to be afraid of me. That is something I really needed to know. As soon as you can get here, come to me so I can tape your shoes."

"I promise, Coach," I worked to fight back the tears.

"Talk to me right away next time you have a problem, Soccer Boy! It is going to be harder to win without you."

Saturday morning approached quickly. I grabbed my box of gum. How I wished I was free to go straight to the game.

"They need me!"

As I was leaving, Mama said, "Take Mario with you today. I think he is almost old enough to learn how to work the docks." It was music to my ears!

The two of us ran to the ocean as if hurrying down there would make the tourist-filled Dories' arrive any sooner from the anchored cruise ships! I actually sold more Chiclets than usual, enough to buy a new box to sell, plus a little extra to buy beans and rice. "Hey Mario, it must have been because you are so little and cute. You will be my good luck charm. Run with me to the game."

Past the taco stand, past the plaza, past the Mercado, we took a right. One more block to the field. It looked like the whole town was out there rooting for

Iguanas or Panthers. I had not envisioned such a crowd for our game. Still, it was easy to spot my family, and it made me smile.

Chapter 13: The Challenge

ESPERANZA'S CONTINUING STORY

The big day of our first game finally arrived. Papa and I were up with the sun. He made his special huevos rancheros recipe.

"It will give you energy."

After putting on my black shirt, I tied my hair back, as wisps in the face are most distracting. Walking to the field, nervous teammates and their family joined us. Alejandro looked intense but handsome in his new black baseball cap. He let us know Pedro would be late and placed Julio on the front line.

The referees were waving at Alejandro to come over. "Hey, is that a girl on your team? Are you trying to cause trouble? You know this game is just for boys. Girls are supposed to cheer the boys on."

Coach reached into his back pocket and pulled out the rulebook. "Show me where it says the girls are not allowed! You know that it is not even mentioned. The rules are the rules."

I was listening to them from the sidelines. When they began nodding, I let out a big sigh of relief.

Coach called Marcos over to the middle of the field. He had won our team's vote as the most improved player which made him team captain for this first game. We could tell he was not expecting the honor because there were tiny tears in his eyes as Coach placed the yellow band on his arm.

The Iguana's were better than we expected. It was halftime already with the teams huddled at each side of the field. Coach was frowning and waving his arms at his team. "We should not be losing 2 to zero," Coach exclaimed.

Chapter 14: The Big Effort

PEDRO SPEAKS

As soon as Coach saw me running to the field, he grabbed the duct tape and quickly attached my slippers to my feet.

The whistle blows for the second half. My heart is pounding. This is where I want to be. This is my life. Once on the field, I manage to take the ball downfield past three opponents and sail the ball up and into the right upper corner past the confused goalie. It all happened so quickly that I looked twice to make sure the ball really was in the net. Both cheers and groans covered the field from the sidelines.

After the midfield kickoff, Jesus Ortiz, a yellow-shirted Iguana, dribbled the ball into Panther territory, quickly passing it to another yellow-shirted forward. He shot. The ball hit the top of the goalpost and did not score. All our black-shirted players felt relief. Pepe, our Panther goalie, gave the ball a high kick down the field. I think he kicks so much further now since he was one of the lucky ones given those valued shoes.

Back and forth the ball traveled, each team determined to keep possession. The whistle blew frequently signaling off-sides as each team's intensity made them forget their position on the field. Elbows flying from both sides were duly noted by the referees. Penalties were called, as both teams struggled to win this first game.

Then Juan got the ball and sent a beautiful pass to me without even looking my way. I was able to bring it to the middle and then pass it across the field to Esperanza, who left-footed it in the net for a score.

The score is now two to two. Just one more goal toward the end of this second half would do it.

"Was that the girl?"

"How did a girl do that from so far away, with her left foot?"

"Who let a girl on their team?"

These comments came from bewildered Iguana supporters on the sidelines.

Our Panther supporters just cheered.

The Iguanas now had possession and brought the ball downfield. Jesus Ortiz again received the ball and with a swift instep boot, kicked it hard towards the Panther goal. Marcos jumped and headed the bullet-like shot to Carlos who again headed it down field.

Magnificent save! Our crowd yelled. I took a deep breath of relief.

"Yeah," Francisco yelled the loudest cheer for the great save and an extra hoot and holler for the accurate headers he had taught.

The whistle blows long and loud. Game over! I longed for at least one more minute.

"It's okay team. We did not lose!" Alejandro reassured the team. "You came back. We will win next time we play them. See you Monday at practice back at the beach again so we can keep those legs strong."

The families decided to clasp hands to form a circle around the team. They began chanting, "Panthers are number one!" over, and over. To them, a tie was as good as a win for a first game.

Soccer is everything for my town. We all feel a new energy. For a short time, we can forget our problems and our poverty.

I never want to look back. Soccer is my life. How I would love to tell the USC girl that I finally am on a team of my own.

Esperanza told me that her father said that when Alejandro watches me play, he feels that he is seeing himself again in my speed, determination, and agility. A glimmer of satisfaction, yet the mountain remains unclimbed. The possibilities feel endless.

Chapter 15: The Shoe Challenge

ALEJANDRO'S STORY AGAIN

I was busy planning for our next game in two more weeks. Shoes were going to be a stumbling block, that's for sure. The silver duct-taped shoes could only be temporary. So, as I was riding my bike on the way home to the ranch, I stopped by Our Lady of Hope rectory. I was relieved when Father Duenas answered the door.

"Are you here for confession, my son?" asked Father. "They don't start until 4:00."

"No," was my laughing reply. "I just spent the last three years paying the debt for something I did not even do. I think I am all clear for at least the next ten years. I am actually here to ask your help with my soccer team."

"You want me to pray they will win?"

"Oh no, they will win. Excuse me, Father, it's just that then you would be praying that the other team loses. I think God just enjoys watching the game."

"What then, my son?"

"I'm just asking that you announce at Mass Sunday that our team, the Panthers, cannot be as barefoot as those jungle cats. We need shoes. Old ones, new ones, big ones or small, it does not matter."

"That sounds like a good project. I have done quite a few funerals lately. I know there must be a number of shoes around that are no longer being used. But first I'd better pray on how to say that delicately?"

"Now that is something worth praying for. Could the parishioners bring them to the rectory?"

"Yes. Let me know when the next game is. I don't get out much. I could use a little excitement."

The third team that had formed on the east side of town decided to call themselves the Cobras. We know Cobras are determined, but I decided they would not get the opportunity to bite. I needed to check them out myself.

As I watched their practice, I saw they were a taller team but not as quick and much less disciplined. Discipline is the feature that I believe is the key to victory, creating a team rather than individuals each playing on their side of the field.

At Monday's practice, the Panthers answered all of the quiz questions correctly. Our team was learning how very many rules there are and what an advantage a team has when they know the correct ones. "You can usually stand your ground when you know the rules, but not always, as the referee, unfortunately, has the last word," I instructed.

"I'd just tell him he is wrong," insisted Carlos.

"It's time to explain red cards, young man! Get one of those, and we will be spending private hours together at my avocado orchards holding the pit in that yappie mouth."

Carlos acted as though I was talking to someone else. I couldn't help wondering what made him so bold.

Since our first game, most of the players realized how exciting it was to be a Panther and be known around town as real soccer players. They wore their black shirts everywhere.

"This will be our first encounter with the many taller players that are on the Cobra team. When I saw them, they resembled small trees with only two branches coming off their sides. Can any of you guess what our best approach will be?" I asked.

"How about we decide to grow?" Antonio's eyes were twinkling.

"You do that. Need a stretching board? We'll be glad to accommodate," I teased. "But, in the meantime…"

Juan responded. "Maybe we should stay low to the ground to get between their legs."

"Good guess. Not exactly what I had in mind."

Esperanza piped up, "Concentrate on not letting them get in front of you. Crisscross, sidestep like this. It's just footwork." She maneuvered her example so quickly that it left the boys blinking. *"Don't worry, it gets easier with practice."*

No one said a word. I tried to hide my smile.

We worked harder than ever. The boys found it a little easier to follow a girl's lead, especially when practice proved that the crisscross-sidestep helped them evade each other.

Towards the end of Wednesday's practice, Father Duenas got out of his little red truck carrying a burlap sack over his shoulder. He walked to the middle of the field, looking a little like Santa. The team gathered around and saw that the bag contained shoes. We lined up as the two of us worked until dark fitting shoes and, of course, silver taping them as often as needed. There was even one giant pair, size 12, left over. The team didn't have real soccer shoes yet, but at least they had their feet covered and were ready to go. This was the break they needed.

"Thanks, Father," echoed the team.

"I can't wait for Saturday!" He replied, pulling out two black jerseys from the bottom of the bag. "Luckily *black is all I get to wear. I found these extra ones that were getting a little small around the middle anyway."*

Juan's shirt was dark grey, so Father passed him a new shirt and another to inside-out Pepsi Boy. "This team needs numbers!" I grabbed the duct tape and started creating rather squared off numbers on the back of the shirts. Pedro was first in line because he wanted number 1. I could have guessed!

Chapter 16: A Bad Decision

PEDRO'S STORY

To sell the Chiclets, I have to go to the docks to meet the Tuesday and Saturday cruise ships. During the busiest seasons, there is one on Thursdays also. Ever since cute Mario had come those first two Saturdays, we have earned more money…even enough to put food in the cupboard for later. I spend a lot of time worrying. It felt good to relax a little.

I wished I could skip the cruise stop this Saturday so I could play the whole game. If only it were an option.

Friday's team scrimmage was intense, with Francisco acting as referee. We thought he seems to be enjoying his newly purchased shrill whistle just a little too much.

Alejandro was on the sidelines during the plays, shouting directions until he was hoarse. Carlos kept moving forward. Coach wanted him back to protect the goalie. Was he ever going to listen? That is when Alejandro had an idea. I saw him go over to Francisco's truck and grabbed his long rope out of the bed.

"Come here, Carlos."

Coach tied the rope around the back-fielder's thick waist. The other end he attached to the goal post with his favorite tool, duct tape. Carlos stopped three direct shots at the goalie over the next five plays.

As Alejandro unfastened him, Carlos said, "Okay Coach, I get it."

"Sometimes actions speak louder than words," I heard Coach mutter to himself.

As I was leaving practice, Coach handed me a pair of good-looking Nikes and said "Father was given a pair of running shoes today, and I think they should fit you fine so at least you won't need taping. Get here tomorrow as soon as you can, Mejo."

My father used to call me that affectionate name. It felt good to hear it. "I will do my best," I replied. I couldn't wait to run home in my new shoes. I knew they could go fast.

Next morning, Mario was awake even before I opened my eyes. "Get up, brother," he said.

While Mama was making the tortillas, we got ready. "I don't want my Pele playing on an empty stomach. I'll see you at the game. Try to hurry," says Mama. She knew we would.

Today as we waited impatiently at the dock, the anchored cruise ships seemed to take forever getting the passengers into the dories so the little boats could bring their customers ashore. One by one, the tourists began stepping onto the dock. Tall, short, young, older, skinny, and plump, all were potential Chiclets customers for us. As the sunburned and tanned faces approached, many were stopping to look at Mario, who was learning to work his audience with those big round eyes and the famous Garcia deep dimples.

"Mario, you are selling more Chiclets than I ever could. Mind if I run back to the game and you can follow when you are done?" I figured Coach would be happy, and besides, Mama did tell me to hurry. Mario nodded yes but looked worried. At six years old, he had never been out of his neighborhood alone.

I was able to run faster to this game in my next-to-new sneakers and got there in the middle of the first half, feeling very clever indeed. Coach was happy to see me so early and put me right into the game. That was rewarding enough.

I was told the game had been delayed 5 minutes because the Cobras protested that the Panthers included a girl on the team. Alejandro had to get out the rulebook again to show that there was no specific rule against girls. The Cobras were not satisfied. The referee sternly announced that the rules are the rules, so the game finally began.

I was delighted to hear that the game was still 0-0. Surprisingly three of the boys were even taller than I had expected. "Good thing we are good at the crisscrosses," I said to Esperanza, taking my position next to her on the field.

There was even a larger crowd than two weeks ago. I noticed Father Duenas was standing at center field line in order not to show favoritism. I figured that if he didn't cheer for both sides, it could affect the collection next Sunday.

Tall does not mean fast, I soon decided. It looks like their legs might have grown faster than their brains could figure out where their legs should go. Kind of like flamingos trying to take flight.

Anxious to get the ball, I want to take it and charge away until I see it score in the goal because that feels more natural to me. With some initial resistance, I began to really listen to Coach and now understand that teamwork and not over aggression will get us to championships. Instead, I have worked on sharpening my skills in order to know where my teammates are, most of the time. Both Alejandro and Francisco kept pushing us to chatter so we will have another tool to locate the best pass.

Marcos gave the ball a swift kick to Antonio who brought it up near the sideline. He trapped the ball, pulled back a step, and shot high over the middle. Esperanza was waiting. This gave her an opportunity for a powerful header to the right, over the goalie's shoulder and into the waiting net.

The Cobras and their fans were sure a girl should not and could not do that. Either way, the score was 1-0.

At the same time, cheers came from the Panther crowd.

The green jersey boys kept the ball at the Panther end for what seemed like an eternity. Marcos, Carlos, and Ramon worked up a sweat defending their goal. They finally got the ball to Pablo, the midfielder, who slowed and controlled the ball with his left foot. There were two Cobras on him. He heard me calling to him and remembered this was a heads-up that another player was in the open and able to receive a pass. He spotted my position, pivoted and shot the ball between four Cobra legs.

I was unguarded and ready. With even more agility than in the past, I received the ball just past midfield, dribbled forward through two out of position defenders and shot hard. The curving ball zinged just out of reach of the goalie's outstretched fingers. Score!

"How did I do that so easily?" I could not keep from commenting to myself. "Guess it was because too many were guarding Pablo, just like coach says"

Juan scored the next goal, two minutes before halftime after Antonio placed a perfect corner kick that practically kissed Juan waiting foot.

Right after the whistle blew, I looked up and saw my mother. What was she doing on this side of our field?

"Where is Mario?" says Mama.

"He will be coming soon," I replied.

"Pedro!" was her shocked reply.

Coach gathered the team together during the break. He was happy. "I think we are gelling, team. Keep it up."

We scored two more goals in the second half. I, Pedro Hernandez Garcia, scored one of them with my first ever heel kick. I could not imagine feeling happier. The Cobras scored one. As the game ended, 5 to 1, I saw Mario running onto the field, his face full of blood.

"What happened?" I shouted, running up to my brother. I quickly took off my shirt to catch the blood spurting from my brother's swollen nose.

"Two big guys I never saw before were waiting at the docks until I was done. Pedro, I grabbed the money tight. I wouldn't let them have it. I ran as fast as I could, but they caught me before I got to the plaza," he said between sobs.

"They got the money, but I bit one of their hands before they ran away." Mario cried. "That's about the time they hit me in the face, I guess. Brother, I sold a lot of the Chiclets today, but I still had some left. I tried to hide the box under my shirt, honest I did. Now we have no Chiclets to sell."

That is when Mama came running back across the field. "Why did you leave your little brother?" she scolded. "That was very selfish. I am disappointed in you, Pedro."

I felt confused. How can I have the best day ever on the same day as almost the worse day ever? The little guy did not deserve this.

We hurried home once the bleeding stopped. My mother didn't speak. Her quietness was as loud as cannon fire. Today's win had lost much of its glory.

Chapter 17: Capture!

PEDRO'S HAPPY TALE

An hour later, there was a knock on the door. Mama answered. Francisco stood tall with each hand pulling on the collar of two scruffy looking boys. Esperanza was standing in the background looking triumphant.

"I found these hooligans at the Mercado buying candy. There is still blood on their shirts. Not smart boys! Please bring Mario out here," said the booming voice of Francisco.

"It was not us," the boys started yelling.

"I wasn't asking you!" Francisco twisted their collars even tighter. While he was pulling them closer, he noticed teeth marks, still indented, on the smaller thief's right hand.

"Are these the boys?" Francisco asked.

Mario, with his new big nose, nodded 'yes' and quickly averted their eyes.

"Empty your pockets now, you thieves."

Many coins spilled from the inside-out pockets. I quickly stepped outside to scoop them up.

"If you do not want this reported to the police, you had better have the gum returned by sundown," barked the assistant coach, as the boys hurried away.

Mama had a grateful smile back on her face.

"Pedro, you are lucky to have such a beautiful mother. Reminds me of Esperanza's mother when she was alive. Be good to her and don't give her worries."

I could not look in his eyes.

I never knew that Francisco didn't notice because his eyes were only on Mama Maria.

All I could do was to lie in our bed against my pillow to hide the tears for all the trouble I had caused.

At Monday's practice, Coach was all smiles. "Good start! No big heads! We are not great yet...only on the way to being great. Big heads just get in the way!"

The team nodded.

"I got a call from my friend, Jorge in El Rosario." Coach said. "We have always been competitors since 8th grade. Jorge coaches a championship team, The Hurricanes. He boasts that his team will show us how foolish we will look. I told him that when we meet, prepare to be surprised.

One difficulty is we need soccer shoes but more than that, we don't have transportation. I will be working on that."

"Wow, I've never been to another town." Pedro thought about all the people from the cruise ships and the different towns they come from. What do other towns look like?

Meanwhile, the team cheered with excitement at the thought of bigger and better challenges.

Chapter 18: I Love Soccer!

PEDRO'S STORY

What a day yesterday was!

I, Pedro Hernandez Garcia, woke early. Since becoming a member of a real soccer team, it was usually my special time to daydream of my future successes, but in truth, I was awake earlier than usual because I had been jabbed in the head by restless Mario one too many times in our crowded bed. Mario must be having nightmares since his beating by the "gum robbers" yesterday.

I felt so guilty at leaving my little brother alone to fend for himself while I ran off to play soccer. The guilt seemed less when I hid my head under my pillow.

Within seconds, I had to come up for air and looked over Mario's face to survey the damages. My 6-year-old brother still had a nose twice as big as the day before, and a black shiner was starting under his puffy right eye. His lower right jaw had a 2-inch scratch, which added to his lopsided look. With relief, I noted that his puffy nose looked straight and he seemed to be breathing easily enough…though his snore was louder than usual.

Since our assistant coach Francisco had caught the boys who stole the money, I hurried to the door to see if they had returned the supply of gum that Mario was selling. Yes, there it was. One-half box of Chiclets right next to our brown front door.

As I was carrying our merchandise back inside, I decided that the robbers probably wouldn't have had the time to think up so many ways of causing trouble if they had been on a soccer team.

In the quiet of the morning, I was able to think about yesterday's soccer game. I was glad that my team, the Panthers, had won and that I had scored two goals and had two assists. But now I needed to concentrate on what I had to do to be the best.

From watching the games through the windows outside The Amigos Bar, I recognized that toward the end of the games, our National Team would look a little tired. The players showed effort in moving their legs as skillfully as earlier in the game. This was especially true if they needed to play overtime when they tied. That is a lot of running. I will run more, I resolved. My brain promised my legs that if I trained hard, they would not tire quickly.

I was also very impressed how quickly these pros could change their direction. "I thought I could turn quickly but not as fast as I'd like, especially after watching these players."

I went out back where Mama and I were collecting bricks for a better house some day. We had 45 yellow bricks stacked in two neat piles. Grabbing a shovel, I loosened the dirt and placed 10 of the bricks together in a straight line, packing the dirt around the edges of each one. I used the remaining bricks to form five brick angles off that line. Starting at the beginning, I then went down the line, angling seven bricks at each offshoot and then on to the next one. It looks a little like a Christmas tree pattern.

"Whew, that is harder than it looks," I said, slightly out of breath.

Mama came outside just as I was finishing the placements.

"Mama, I was wrong yesterday. I am sorry."

"I know you are, Son. Let it never happen again."

As she patted me on the head, I realized that she was working on forgiving me for abandoning my brother and I felt happy.

I explained my brick running technique. "Well, I am delighted that these bricks now have a job to do while they are waiting to become a house!" was her smiling response. "Let me be the first to watch you demonstrate, Mr. Pele." It took a real turning of my feet to get to the end. I think my invention is going to work well.

Two hours later, Francisco came by and asked us how Mario was doing. I noticed that he had his hair slicked back, was wearing a starched plaid shirt and some kind of aftershave. He smelled like a woman as he passed by. I couldn't hear their conversation, but it seemed that this man was taking up quite a lot of time for so few questions. And why was Mama smiling at everything he said? He had never seemed so funny to me. She even showed him our new training gizmo.

As Francisco was leaving, I walked up to this tall man to thank him again for helping our family deal with those rough boys. "Just try to do your best in life, and don't make your mother worry, Pedro."

"Yes, sir!"

Chapter 19: The Avocado Plan

ALEJANDRO'S STORY AGAIN

Working at the avocado ranch, the first avocado trees were ready to be picked in another week, and Uncle Santos was concerned about getting it all done while his crop was at perfect ripeness. His older brothers usually helped but they were becoming more bent over every year, and slower too.

Alejandro told his uncle that he just thought of a plan. "My team can help you pick the fruit and load it on the truck. The team will take it to the grocery warehouse 10 miles outside Ensenada. You will then let us take the truck further into Ensenada where we can play Jorge Mejia's winning team. That would be our pay, which would include dinner after the game, as I believe the team will be quite starving by then."

"Sounds like a plan," said Uncle Santos. "It's a go if I can go too. You know how temperamental 'Andy' the truck can be. He is used to me as the driver, after our 20 years together. Anyway, I could use a change of scenery because these avocados have no personality. I talk to them, but they never say anything back."

He called a meeting on Tuesday with the boys and their parents so he could arrange a Friday workday followed by the produce delivery and on to the game on Saturday. He also had gone to the school, talked with the principal, and arranged the day off in exchange for an extra hour of class each day during the next week.

Pedro told him that his family all decided to go to the docks on Saturday morning to sell the Chiclets so he would not miss the game! Alejandro felt relief! He decided all those little smiling faces could even help sales.

The team was told all they would each need was a packed lunch. They were so excited about the idea of an out of town game followed by a real restaurant dinner that our day of work sounded like a fair trade. The players all felt they were on their way to being famous!

Not surprisingly, Carlos announced that he did not like climbing things and would only pick the avocados he could reach from the ground. He seemed too tough to have a fear of heights, or was this a trick to keep his workload light?

Alejandro frowned, not Carlos again! He knew team unity is a must. Coach thanked this stubborn one for 'volunteering' to pick up all the avocados on the ground, as he laughingly realized that bending over that many times can be more difficult and would take longer than everyone else. Maybe Carlos would learn soon, or maybe he preferred to learn slowly. Time would tell.

During that next week, Alejando was a little late for practice as he worked to get ready for harvest. What a curious road has led him to this time of my life he thought, as he drove the old tractor past the last row of fruit-laden trees.

Chapter 20: Eye on the Goal

BACK TO ESPERANZA'S STORY

Practice was intense during the following week. Alejandro instructed us, "The Hurricanes have the advantage of having played together for the past 18 months." Alejandro instructed. "Their coach, my friend, has a personal agenda to scare us. He boosts that his unbeaten team is not only fast, but they are known for their sliders from the sides."

I couldn't wait to say, "Don't forget they don't know about our crisscross. Sliders don't work well if we perfect the crisscross. And meanwhile, they will be on the ground more often with their famous fanny sliders.

Fortunately, our team decided to get right to the business of perfecting my crisscross. We also worked hard on left foot kicking and even harder on getting the ball away from me. Not so easy, is it?

It had taken me quite a while to be treated as one of the guys, and I wonder at times if it is me or the coach's warning. Either way, I plan to outshine them all eventually, which will make my point.

My father announced that Tuesday's practice was going to be extra long.

"Why?" we asked.

"You'll see. Don't worry. I'll bring some snacks for everyone, so you don't fade away."

That Monday night we were more tired than usual. What could possibly be harder?

Even Alejandro questioned what plan Francisco had in mind. "Wait and see," I heard Francisco reply.

School seemed to last a long time on Tuesday, and Pedro seemed extra late getting to school. It must have been lucky sales day. I find myself looking forward to his handsome face.

I have started to make extra notes for him on what he missed in class. This is part of what teamwork is all about, I decided.

On arriving at the field on Tuesday, we saw that my Francisco had placed a 6-foot long beam that was only 4-inches wide, up on concrete blocks at the left side of the field. I noticed that he had safely anchored the apparatus to the ground with stakes.

"Today I want each of you to practice walking on the balance bar, first forward and then backward," says Francisco. "I will time you so you can see your progress. This is only the first lesson on this beam as I want you to become more advanced in your balance."

"What are we, sissy ballerinas?" grunted Carlos under his breath but heard by the assistant coach.

"Oh, Carlos, did you just say you want to go first? Step right up, Bro." Everyone stifled a laugh as he teetered on the beam. "Get back on the field," he commanded to the rest of the team. "Carlos and I have some work to do here. Each of you will have a turn."

Carlos' first attempt was daunting. Why was it so difficult? Francisco picked up a stick. "Hold the other end with your left hand. It will help you until you get used to it." Carlos, of course, hesitated. Macho boys don't need help. After a few sorry attempts, he grabbed the end from his mentor and navigated rather smoothly to the end. Three more guided lengths and Carlos felt ready for a solo. He waved away the stick and made it to the end with a minimum of wobbles. "Coach, I can see this is going to help my balance," Carlos said in a quiet breath.

"The Olympics are starting in a few months. I will be able to show you the male gymnasts. It would be impossible to call them sissies. Two more lengths young man, then you can return to the field."

"That looks like an excellent training technique, Francisco." smiled Alejandro." Who wants to be next?"

One by one, I saw the boys struggle and then improve their beam walks. When it was Pedro's turn, his legs looked unsure. He said it was fun, but he looked forward to more practice.

I was last, walking backward and forward with ease, not resisting doing one flip right before a perfect back somersault dismount.

I decided to keep my other maneuvers under my hat as I still wanted to stay one of the boys for now.

Chapter 21: The Big Avocado Pick

PEDRO'S Story

Before practice was over, Mr. Rios, the owner of the Amigos Bar, walked onto the field. "What is he doing here?" I asked Juan. "Is he going to scold us for peeking on his windows on soccer game days?"

Mr. Rios was a heavy, tall man with wild hair and bushy grey mustache who we never saw except through the dark window.

"Hello, boys, ah, ah, and girl. I stopped by to tell you that I have heard how well your team is doing. I have seen you peeking through my window for quite a while during the National games. I want you to be able to see the best up close. Business has improved lately, and I have decided to purchase a second television for The Amigos bar. Wear your team shirts, and I will include a free soda with each game. I want you to study every move these players make. You have two expert coaches. I expect great things from you. Soon our town will be known as the best soccer town, and I want to help make it happen."

He then reached into his bag and pulled out a new soccer ball with 'Amigos Bar' hand imprinted in red on both sides. "I also have an extra water cooler that will be larger and keep the water cooler on the hot days. Now don't disappoint me, boys, ah, ah, I mean team," looking over uncomfortably at Esperanza's shining face.

We all let out war hoops, claps and yells. Is this what getting famous would feel like?

Friday arrived bright and a little too sunny. Alejandro picked up five of our team at school, drove them in his car. Francisco stuffed the rest of us into the back of his pickup and dropped us off on his way to work. "I'll be back to get you at 4:00 on my way home."

"Today you are going to do hard work. When you are grown and have a difficult job, I hope you will all still have soccer in your lives that will keep smiles on your faces. Are you ready?" asked Francisco?

Mrs. Rocha hurried out of the school with a large brown bag of pan dolce as they were about to leave. "I thought you may need a little boost to get you started." She was greeted with eager smiles.

Uncle Santos was waiting at the ranch wearing his beat-up cowboy hat. "Pick the big green ones. If they feel stuck still to the branch, leave them until the second harvest in two weeks. Most should be ready now. Pair up. One of you can hold the ladder for the climber. Switch off whenever you move the ladder to the next tree. The new water cooler is under the palm tree. Don't forget to drink lots of water to stay hydrated. Lunch hour will be at noon."

By 3:30, the trees had their first pick complete. It seemed like a long day. When Alejandro looked at the old truck half loaded with bins of avocados, he felt proud of his new farmers.

"You will all sleep well tonight. Be at the field by 7:30 tomorrow," instructed Coach. "The game will start at 2:00 sharp on the high school field in Ensenada. Since it is far from here, tell your parents we will not start home until after dinner."

The team was almost too tired to respond.

Chapter 22: Fighting with Andy

ALEJANDRO SAYS

I hardly slept that Friday night. Play after play ran through my head. Have I done enough? Will my ragtag team be able to score against this well-known team? Am I expecting too much since we have only played two games so far? Have I put myself in the position of being a laughingstock in front of this challenging friend? Sleep finally prevailed.

As the sun was showing itself above the horizon, I heard the blue Andy truck rattling up the road toward our schoolyard. Everyone was there, ready to board for the big game. Parents were excited about the team and cheered them on. This was a big day for everyone.

The boys and Esperanza climbed into the back of the truck each clenching their lunch bags. I pulled the back gate closed. It popped open. I closed it again. It popped open, again!

"I need the team to move toward the front of the truck bed, please," I shouted. "We need more space for an extra forceful push." That was tricky for them as the avocados were definitely in the way.

A big clank followed. Pop! Andy's door gave way and pulled open again. Uncle Santos and Francisco got out of the cab and tried closing it from the outside. No luck. The door did not want to stay closed.

"Time for your famous duct tape, Coach," Pedro yelled out. I reached into gym bag and pulled out his magic roll, twisting it around and around the gate opening and the post. "I hope you brought scissors so we can get the bins out.", Juan shouted out.

"That's why I always have my Swiss Army knife. It has a tool for everything."

Off to the warehouse first!

The backends of trucks are often used for travel in Mexico. The more, the merrier as most families don't have cars.

Juan started singing, and soon we thought we sounded like the group One Direction, traveling down the road. What we didn't have in talent was made up for in volume. Even the cows on the side of the road looked up.

An hour later, Uncle Santos steered Andy down a long gravel road. The exaggerated bumps woke Marcos who had been slumped against one of the bins. "Where am I?" he growled. The boys thought that was very funny and quickly slipped one of their black shirts over his head. "Guess, guess, maybe you are in Texas. Maybe you are still home in bed, Sleepyhead." Marco being the strongest one, quickly removed the homemade mask and threw an avocado at the perceived tormentor. As luck would have it, it was overripe, as demonstrated when It split, and squished all over me after Philippe ducked under the green weapon. Marcos' eyes became as big as saucers and fear filled all their faces.

Silence followed.

I looked stern and then laughed. "We all make mistakes Marcos. That doesn't mean I won't get you back later, Dude."

Relief was evident. No one wants to make me mad.

Due to the many hands, the avocados were taken off the truck and out of the bins in record time after cutting the duct tape. The gruff manager gave Santos the money, and the team returned to the truck bed. The empty crates, piled higher, created more room. Now our legs could stretch out.

Rumbling Andy was on his way! Ten more minutes into the journey, all seemed to be going as scheduled.

A large thud!

What happened!

The truck bed felt katty-whompus.

On the narrowest part of the gravel road, way past the warehouse, an unseen pothole was hidden in the high weeds. Andy discovered the ditch with his back-right tire.

Not now! Game time was in two hours, and we had another hour of travel.

"Everybody off the truck! Jump over the sides, so we don't have to mess with the tape right now."

"Darn!" yelled Francisco. "Good that only one wheel went in. I wish you were not so big, Mr. Andy. Let's get pushing. We need all your muscles."

We pushed and pushed until sweat broke out but no luck.

"We need a plank," said Santos. "Break down one of the crates and that should help."

They pulled off a crate, and I started kicking it. It gave me great pleasure to be able to get rid of some of his frustration. Alfonso grabbed one of the boards and handed another to Carlos. "Pull some of this dirt away from the front off the wheel so the tire will have a better chance to grip."

"Now let's get out of the rut." Carlos' strong arms turned the wood into a shovel. We noted that he did not complain this time. Meanwhile, I was able to duct tape two boards together to make a stronger plank to support the weight of the wheel.

"One more big try. Rev it up easy," we called to Santos.

Everyone held their breath as we gave Andy our biggest effort. He groaned and squeaked and whirled but slowly and surely, he fishtailed his way back onto the road, greeted by loudest of cheers. Carlos took a well-deserved bow. For once, he was not causing trouble. I thought he even seemed to be enjoying his new role.

One hour wasted, we were finally on our way.

"Better start on your lunches now."

I did not have to say it twice as I poured water from the new jug.

"I wonder what Ensenada will look like. I've only seen pictures." I said between bites. "Lots of cars, traffic lights and noise, I think," replied Juan.

Esperanza chimed in, "Yes, it has its good and bad, but it is more exciting than our town, that's for sure. When we lived in Guadalajara, people seemed more dressed up and fashion conscious. I miss that part."

The boys did not get why anyone would miss that. They responded with silence.

The roar of Andy's engine and full stomachs signaled a short nap for most of them. No sleep was possible for me. How was I going to direct these scruffy boys to play against a team that has played many teams and consistently won? Maybe I was too anxious in betting against his old friend and rival. It would be hard on the team's egos if they got shut out on their first away game.

Pedro was also awake. I could almost see the thoughts scurrying around his brain. He moved closer to me and whispered, "This dream is so big in me, sometimes I think I could explode. I feel so excited about my future but so scared, at the same time, that I might fail. Scared that I will let my team down. Scared that I will let my family down. I can't let my dream go away." He sighed and took a deep breath. "I will ask Papa to give me strength. He was so strong and so good to us. I will use his strength." Another deep breath. "I can do it. Thanks, Papa."

I saw again where coaching gives me a chance to help change lives.

Andy entered the town, taking up more than his share of the road. "Wake up Panthers! Take a look! This is Ensenada. We will be at the Hurricanes' field soon. We will have an hour to stretch and get ready."

Ten minutes of turns and twists down crowded streets ended at a larger greener field than they had ever seen. A big blue flag with THE HURRICANES imprinted on it, greeted us. I could feel my body tense. We could see on the other side of the field their 22 boys all dressed in professional blue and white spanking clean uniforms, high socks with shin guards and brand-new looking soccer shoes.

Chapter 23: Are We Ready?

ALEJANDRO'S WORDS

Visualizing how our twelve-player team would be presenting their second-hand scruffy selves, I suddenly had the urge to hunker down in the bed of the truck and yell to Santos to keep driving. Instead, I took a deep breath as we approached the parking lot. The large lump in my stomach finally seemed to dwindle as the vehicle came to a stop.

"Ok, everyone out."

Looking up, I had the best surprise in a very long time. There stood my brother Beto, smiling ear to ear. How did you know I was here?" asked the astounded brother.

"A little bird told me."

"Was his name Santos?"

"Could be and he also told me that the team did not have long socks or shin guards. This city does not allow games to be played without them. Papa took up a collection among the family and friends for the Panthers. Lucky he could get them at cost. He really believes in you, Alejandro."

"That is good to hear. What a break for us! Line the boys up."

"Wait, that player is too pretty to be a boy, Alejandro."

"You are very observant. You may not have a leg, but you are not blind," teased Coach.

Beto frowned. "This may be a problem. Do you want to start the game with trouble?"

"No of course not, but the rule book says nothing about prohibiting girls and Beto wait till you see her play! This controversy is not new to me. I can handle it."

After presenting the excited team with the shin protectors and black socks, Francisco directed the warm-up.

Beto and I crossed the field and then were greeted by Coach Jorge Mejia, who was looking as arrogant as ever. Though he was short in stature, he made up for it by his bulldog manner.

"Good thing we have loved you all these years in spite of yourself, Amigo," smiled Beto.

"Great to see you too, but it'll be even better when we crush you. Hey, is that a girl I see out there? Shouldn't you be named The Sissy Team?"

"Stop right there!" I commanded with my arms on my hips, my eyes glaring, just to look determined.

"There is no rule in the rule book against females. Until they change it, they have every right to play. Enough said!"

Jorge knows me well enough to know when to let the big guy have the last word about a subject.

"Your team really looks poor," Jorge bellowed out-loud.

"They are very poor but do not confuse that with weakness. Though our team has not played many games, they are well trained and full of spirit. Your more pampered players may never have needed to gather that kind of strength. Besides, they don't feel poor because they have me."

As they returned to the team, Beto laughed at the two of us who he said sounded like we had returned to high school days.

I hurried to gather the team around me, "Do not let their spunky looks intimidate you. They have to wear those perfect uniforms to cover their lumpy sugar filled bodies,"

The team liked that thought.

"Maybe they will cry to Mama if they get dirt on them!"

"They probably don't know how to do a super fast crisscross."

"They probably have never even played in the sand."

Confidence was rising and very needed.

"Ten minutes to kickoff. You all know your positions. Do not, I repeat, do not let yourselves get distracted or intimidated. Constantly visualize the ball going through the goal. If you say I probably won't make it or there's no way we can win, well guess what? That ball will follow your stink thinking."

"I want everyone to take three deep cleansing breaths like I taught you. Ask God to help you stay alert. You are ready.

I need to go give the refs your names and ages."

I handed the list to the head referee and said, "Before you ask, because I know you will, yes there is a girl on my team. Yes, it is unusual. No, there is no written rule against it." I was hoping this approach would keep the game from being delayed.

"It is indeed unusual. As long as you know she could get hurt."

"So, could any of my players. Believe me, she can hold her own."

The refs shrugged.

A whistle finally started the long-anticipated game.

"I am glad we are equal in size to this Hurricane team." noted Francisco as the team positioned for kickoff. "We do not have as many subs as they do. Good thing our team is used to running."

Juan was first to the ball, passing it to Esperanza who crisscrossed it around and past two Blues. With her ponytail flying, she kicked it to me. I rushed past a big defender and left foot kicked it high, towards the right front corner of the net. An awesome save was made by the orange-attired Hurricane goalie. He reached up to deflect the ball just before landing in a belly flop as the ball bounced back into play.

Both teams became aware that they had their work cut out for them this warm afternoon. The Blues were finding that the country bumpkins were fiercer than they appeared. Maybe it would not be the easy win that Coach Mejia had outlined for them.

We Panthers were well aware of the Hurricane's ability to score quickly.

Then the Hurricanes played triangle passes downfield that appeared too swift for comfort until their number 7 met Marcos. He was ready and charged after that ball as if it was a bomb. He kicked the ball out from between number 7's feet, and it went to midfield. Philippe got the pass. With two opponents on him, he saw that Pedro was open and was calling to him. He stiffened his arm toward these opponents and right footed the shiny ball in front of me.

Instinct must have taken over as Pedro stepped up and charged the net sending a rocket ball to the left lower corner with such a force that it was almost unseen from the sidelines. Score! 1 to 0!

Sweat broke out on the goalie's brow after he just missed blocking the corner.

Santos was seen giving a high five and jumping higher than he had in years.

The plays continued. The Hurricanes pushed with their bodies a little more than the Panthers were used to, but it did not take long before they met force with force. Carlos took it all a little too seriously and got a yellow card as he dove for the ball and hit the knee of the defensive player just before halftime.

The Hurricane's striker sent a beautiful header to his forward, and the team moved toward the goal with the forward midfielder right footing the ball into the goal. Whistle. Offsides! Goal called back. Immense groaning from the sidelines.

Francisco was biting the side of his hand just before a look of relief followed.

Pepe readjusted his goalie gloves and stretched in the net determined to be ready for the next assault.

The plays continued with much yelling and directing from the sidelines. Number 11, a short player with hair that looked like it had to cover his eyes, tripped Philippe and sent him sprawling. No penalty was called. OK, play on. It took a minute for Philippe to get his land legs back.

Tomas was ticked and stole the ball from the Hurricane striker, swooping around one of their slower players. He popped the ball forward, and Esperanza headed it in past the straining goalie as if she were using a racket. It sailed over the Blues' heads and dropped sharply into the goal just like she had practiced daily.

Two to zero.

Two minutes later, the halftime whistle blew.

Immediately Coach Jorge was heard yelling at his Hurricanes, "How could you let a mere girl get that goal? Are you afraid to guard her? You will have to personally answer to me if she is allowed any more points."

He continued yelling. "Most of all watch number 1. Do not let that number 1 out of your sight. He is a deadly shot."

We loved hearing that! We all looked at Pedro and gave him a high five.

"I think the midfield will be their weakness. I want you to press down and get to the middle as soon as you can. Don't be gentle. You were overconfident, and that could have been my fault, knowing too much about this team. Time to end this confidence unless you like losing!" Jorge Mejia growled.

Meanwhile, I brought the team under the shade tree. "Do not let up, no matter what. They are waiting to find a kink in our armor. 2 to 0 can change in a flash. I'm sure they will be fired up by the time they are sent back on the field."

"We can hear they are getting the big lecture about being overconfident. As you can tell by their quick moves, they are a strong, well-trained team. Now it is up to us to be better! "

"Hey Juan, I haven't seen you drink any water this halftime. You know how important I have told you hydration is. Why are you not following my directions?"

"Coach I just have to pee so bad I don't dare drink any."

"Beto come over here. Please drive 'little bladder' to the nearest shop and get back here as fast as you can."

"Julio will take your position for now."

"I think I can hold it," said Juan with a look of concentration.

"Do as you are told, Mejo, right now."

"Finish your water team. Time to get back to winning that ball!"

Play speeded up to a frantic pace. The Hurricanes maneuvered the ball near their goal. Blues and Blacks bunched in front of the net. The ball bounced up and hit Carlos' moving arm. The referee's whistle stopped the game. A hand ball in the goal. Bad news!

The Panthers lined up across the field, looking as fierce as possible in their many shades of black. Number 14 blue stepped up to the ball. It seemed to have a life of its own as it sailed under the middle of the upper bar.

2 to 1 now! Carlos gave the grass one swift kick as he returned to kickoff.

It seemed like cheering from the blue supporters would not end.

The afternoon was getting hotter, as was the action. Julio received the ball from Antonio, trapping it before he booted it into the goal. The goalie looked like he was about to fumble the twirling ball when he managed to grasp it in his gloved hands.

Julio tried to hide a smile after his effort. Felt better than sitting on the bench. It was closest to a score he had in any game. Next time he would put it in for sure.

He looked toward Coach and saw that Juan had returned. After being waved-in, he reluctantly walked back to the bench.

PEDRO'S POINT OF VIEW

The Hurricanes seemed to be keeping the ball near their scoring goal entirely too long. They were giving Carlos, Marco, and Pepe a workout that their previous losing teams had not been able to conquer. There were two corner kicks in a row for the blues. I held my breath as the ball was saved from the goal.

Twice, our blacks jumped high and used those over-practiced headers to keep the blues from scoring.

Beto kept yelling, "Bring that ball down to the right! Stop the Hurricanes!"

Antonio was able to dribble the ball past midfield to Juan. With his eye on me, perfectly positioned in the line of the goal, Juan popped the ball directly to me. Gangly Hurricane number 4 pulled a slide tackle maneuver and won the ball before it reached his waiting foot. I was used to slide tackles but had never seen one done with that kind of swift precision. I had to pull back my own arm, as a tempting swift jab in his back could have ended that play for the blue jersey. Lucky I was aware that would have also produced a costly foul on me.

"I will not let that happen again!" I promised myself. Minutes later, I slid my right leg between the legs of the next defender, knocking it from between those legs straight to Esperanza. Soccer lovers call this a 'nutmeg move' I reminded myself.

"That is much better!" I decided.

Esperanza crisscrossed past a huge midfielder, balanced perfectly on the toes of her left foot and shot, scoring again, this time under the goalie's left leg.

Boos and cries of "not that girl again" erupted from the sideline. The Panthers couldn't have cared less about their complaints.

Esperanza and I gave each other a high five. 3 to 1 sounded better than ever!

Hurricanes became rougher. There were two definite fouls that were not called, but Coach had already warned us that can happen when we play home teams.

They had a corner kick, and their well-experienced team lined up determined to score. And score they did. Pepe's fingertips touched the ball, but he only slowed it. I saw that he just could not grasp it.

3 to 2! Too close! Our Panthers felt anxious as we relined at midfield. I felt only excitement. "We can do this."

The ball was flying, bodies were careening against each other. Time was running out; patience was running short.

Felix, our midfielder, was tripped so deliberately that he flew three feet, landing flat on his stomach, compelling the referee to finally give their offender a yellow card. Booing was heard from their sideline. We just shook our heads.

Hurricanes backed up as Felix finally stood up and kicked the ball down the midfield. I kept my eye on number 4 this time. I figured if I kept him in my vision on my left, he could not blindside from the right again as he increased his speed. I reached the spinning ball and without hesitation dribbled in a back and forth motion that both defenders had difficulty tracking. Two seconds later, my kick sounded so right to my ears as it left my shoe and entered the net on the opposite side of the waiting goalie. I remember thinking, "That one was for you, Papa!"

The clock ran out, the whistle blew with the final score 4 to 2.

Alejandro blinked away his moist eyes, Francisco jumped in delight, Santos ran out on the field (the most running he had done in years), and Beto looked at his brother with pride.

The team was jubilant and lined up to shake hands with the Hurricanes. They had to wait on the field while Coach Mejia insisted his elite team be good losers.

Jorge walked over to the scraggly blacks who looked so incapable of beating his unbeatable team. "You have given me some lessons today. It is not how you look, but what you do and how you have been coached that counts," he said, looking at Alejandro.

He looked at Santos asking, "Can you drive the team to the Hacienda Restaurant while Coach, Beto and I go for a quick beer? We will catch up shortly."

"Sure, Francisco and I will meet you there. We can handle it."

Coach told us, on the way home, that once settled at the bar over Coronas, his childhood friend did not look up but stared at the lime. "That was some game, Alejandro. I came to crush you and your little amateur team with my head as big as one of those soccer balls just so everyone here and in Guadalajara would hear of my win. Guess old rivalries die slowly."

We also heard him tell Santos that Jorge said "I will probably only say this once so listen carefully. I know you have had hard times killing your dreams. I do love you, Bro, and I am so proud of you. With the amazing moves your ragamuffins made today, you need to make the goal of professional coaching your life work. Mexico needs people like you and me and Beto and several your players. We need to set our sights on the Olympics and World cup, for our country and ourselves. I know people who can get your team invitations to tournaments and exposure to news media. The rest will be up to you."

He added that Beto chimed in, lifting his bottle, "Amen, my amigos, amen!"

Minutes later, Beto and Alejandro were dropped off at the Hacienda Restaurant and were greeted by clapping and cheering. Coach looked each of us in the eye, "Today, each of you is my hero." He then turned to Esperanza and said, "My friend Jorge told me 'I never thought I would ever see a girl perform so well on a soccer field.' I believe you may have started a revolution and taught me as well."

"A victory dinner always tastes better than a consolation one. Order whatever you want, hungry ones" announced Santos, followed by more cheering.

Alejandro announced that because of our impressive playing, it was almost assured that there would be more out of town games. He was looking right at me when he said it.

My heart felt like it was singing. "I can be Pele or Messi, maybe better."

I was anxious to share the good news with my family but not before filling my waiting stomach!

Acknowledgements:
To my soccer-loving family. Thanks for the kindness, continuing support and encouragement.

Players today…coaches tomorrow.

Made in the USA
San Bernardino, CA
18 November 2019